Grandmother's Song

To Darshana because you are the oldest – love Baba

To my mother and my daughter – J.M.

Barefoot Books
41 Schermerhorn Street, Suite 145
Brooklyn, New York
NY 11201-4845

Graphic design by Design/Section
Color separation by Grafiscan, Verona
Printed in Singapore by Tien Wah Press (Pte) Ltd

ISBN 1 902283 02 3

Library of Congress Cataloging-in-Publication Data available on request

1 3 5 7 9 8 6 4 2

Grandmother's Song

Written *by* Barbara Soros *& Illustrated by* Jackie Morris

BAREFOOT BOOKS

In the heart of Mexico, hawks soar above high mountains and swoop down to gentle slopes of corn below. There on glistening rocks, iguanas rest beneath the hot, tropical sun. Toucans chatter to ring-tailed cats perched in emerald green trees. All through these hills, puma run, grey foxes search for chickens and wolves call to each other in the night.

In a village at the foot of these mountains, a grandmother lived with her granddaughter. They planted corn, tomatoes and sunflowers in the spring and watched as new green shoots sprang from the earth. They gathered milk-white lilies in the summer and put them in baskets on their backs and took them to market. At harvest time, they decorated tall stalks of maize at the corn festival, to give thanks for the year's grain. On the Day of the Dead, they made an altar and lit candles, remembering their loved ones. And at Christmas, they took paper and glue to make piñatas, filling them with fruit and sweets.

Grandmother stood proud and tall. Her downy cheeks stretched smooth and plump across wide cheekbones. Her eyes were deep and warm and brown, and though they were sad, they were also kind. Her breasts were soft and full, and at her hips she was round, all the way around. Powerful legs and sturdy feet rooted her to the earth, like an ancient tree. Her arms were strong and her hands graceful, with long, fine fingers.

Granddaughter was as delicate as the blossoms of a jacaranda tree. Her wide-open eyes shone black and clear. Her tiny, bow lips looked as if she ate strawberries all day long. Granddaughter loved to explore and to imagine. She often played in the fields and forests on her own, but as she played she trembled. For she was afraid of the dark shadows and of the cries of the animals and of anything that was new and strange.

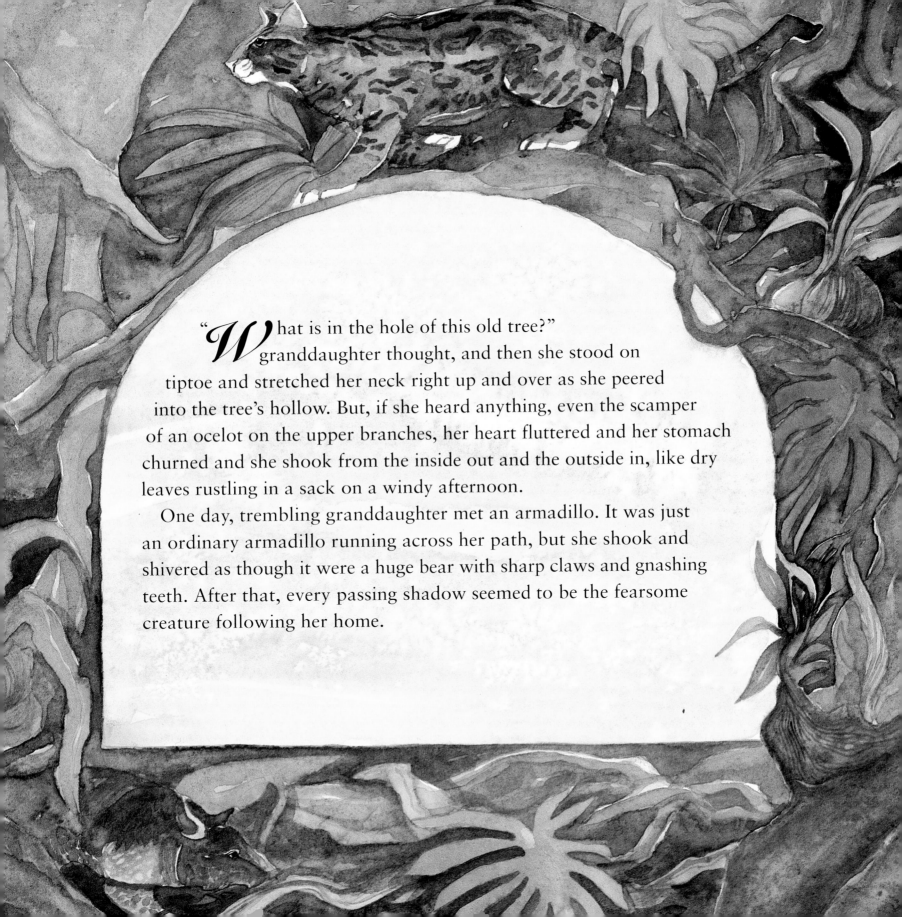

"What is in the hole of this old tree?" granddaughter thought, and then she stood on tiptoe and stretched her neck right up and over as she peered into the tree's hollow. But, if she heard anything, even the scamper of an ocelot on the upper branches, her heart fluttered and her stomach churned and she shook from the inside out and the outside in, like dry leaves rustling in a sack on a windy afternoon.

One day, trembling granddaughter met an armadillo. It was just an ordinary armadillo running across her path, but she shook and shivered as though it were a huge bear with sharp claws and gnashing teeth. After that, every passing shadow seemed to be the fearsome creature following her home.

When grandmother heard the door creak open, she ran to her granddaughter and scooped her up in her arms, hugging her. Then she settled granddaughter on her great, wide lap and gently stroked her. She stroked her head and her slender back, and as she stroked, she sang, "Oh, my little one, I can feel your young heart beating so. I can feel trembling inside your belly. I can hear fear inside your bones."

She stroked and stroked and then continued, "The world is a frightening place for those who cannot trust. So I am stroking trust into you, the trust I feel and the trust my grandmother felt and her grandmother before her."

Granddaughter felt an immense warmth entering her body, and as the sun set behind the house, slowly the trembling eased and she fell asleep.

The next day, a group of children surprised trembling granddaughter while she played at the roadside. They ran over a hill right towards her, gleefully laughing and shouting. "Which way to the river?" they called. Instead of running away, granddaughter pointed to the left without her finger wavering, even though she was shaking inside.

That evening, trembling granddaughter told her grandmother what had happened. Grandmother smiled. "That's progress!" she declared. She lifted granddaughter on to her lap and stroked her like a cat, then she began to sing, "Listen carefully, my little one. I can feel trembling in your belly. I can hear fear inside your bones. The world is a frightening place for those without courage, but today you showed you were brave by pointing the way even though you wanted to run."

With long, loving strokes she caressed her beloved grandchild, and then she continued, "To your own brave act I am adding my bravery and the bravery of my grandmother and her grandmother before her."

Granddaughter felt a surge of strength rush through her body, and the trembling stopped.

Some time later, a young hummingbird fell from a nest in the garden and broke its wing. Instead of running away, trembling granddaughter walked towards the little bird and picked it up. Its body was shaking even more than her own. She could feel its tiny, fluttering heart and its warm, feathery tummy. She held the hummingbird with the same tenderness as her grandmother had held her, and carried it inside.

Grandmother knew how to look after hurt animals. Together they made a little nest of cloth and straw in a box and fed the bird with an eye-dropper. One drop at a time, the young girl dripped clear water into the bird's tiny beak, and as she did so, a thrill ran through her body.

Grandmother's smile spread across her face and lit up her eyes. "Certainly, this is progress!" she exclaimed. And while the hummingbird slept, grandmother took trembling granddaughter on to her broad lap and sang to her, "My little one, listen well. I can feel trembling in your belly. I can hear fear inside your bones. The world is a frightening place for those who cannot help others. Today you helped a tiny, frightened creature and discovered your gift of healing."

All through the night, she held her beloved grandchild safe on her comfortable lap and sang, "This is my gift that I am stroking into you. It is also the gift of my grandmother and of her grandmother before her."

One afternoon, trembling granddaughter was browsing at a market stall when the merchant accused a child of stealing something he had not taken. She watched the angry face of the merchant as he jabbed his finger at the child. Though her heart beat loudly, trembling granddaughter approached the man and said, "This boy did not take anything; I have watched him. Please do not scream at him."

The merchant just snarled in reply, so she asked, "How much money have you lost?"

"Ten pesos," he muttered. The girl reached into her pocket and gave him all her spending money.

"*A*h, this is really progress!" grandmother remarked as trembling granddaughter told her tale, gasping for breath, as she had run all the way home.

Then grandmother took her beloved grandchild on her broad lap and stroked her for a very long time. "My little one, listen well," she sang. "The world is a frightening place for people without dignity. Today you showed your dignity, when you stood tall between the earth and sky. To that I add the dignity I have been given, the dignity of my grandmother and of her grandmother before her."

Trembling granddaughter sensed a strange pride pour through her body. She felt bigger and stronger than usual and her face felt vibrant and warm.

How many times did grandmother stroke granddaughter? How many times did she sing to her? I do not know. But I do know that she did it many, many times, for many weeks and for many years. She stroked trust and courage, skill and dignity into trembling granddaughter. And her song went so deep that it moved through the girl's flesh into her muscles, into her blood, into her heart, and finally into her bones.

Granddaughter grew up to be trusting and trustworthy, generous and kind. No one even remembered that she once ran from armadillos. Soon she grew up into a strong and confident woman, rich in laughter, delighting in everything around her.

Now granddaughter had children of her own, but still, on occasions, she laid her head on grandmother's lap. She understood well the language of grandmother's hands. And so, as the old woman's fingers traced their familiar path, granddaughter smiled and closed her eyes.

In time, grandmother grew old and more frail. So granddaughter attended to her, coming at dawn to light the fire and to boil water for tea. She cooked for her and she washed and brushed her fine, silver hair. She massaged her well-worn feet, gently rubbing every single toe. She took grandmother's loving hands in hers and massaged her old, stiff fingers. Sometimes, but now much less frequently, they walked together across the village, through the valley into the mountains, laughing and singing together. And wherever the ground was uneven, granddaughter offered grandmother her arm.

One night in a dream, grand-daughter saw grandmother walking up the mountains alone. She wanted to walk with her, but grandmother turned and raised her hand. "I have to go on alone," she said, with a quiet smile in her eyes.

The next morning, granddaughter went to grandmother's house as usual. But when she went to wake her, grandmother's body was cold and her face free from worry.

Granddaughter dropped to her knees. Grief struck as quickly and precisely as lightning.

She felt her heart flutter and her stomach churn, just as they had when she was a child. She trembled from head to toe, like cedar branches in a raging storm. How could she live without her beloved grandmother? Her heart opened like a river and tears soaked her face and spilled onto her chest. She doubled over in despair and sobs welled up from her belly and her bones.

"My little one," grandmother's voice filled the room. "My little one, listen well." Granddaughter felt strong, warm hands tenderly stroking her back. These invisible hands felt more immense than grandmother's earthly hands. They stroked well-being into her from her head to her toes, up her front and down her back. She felt the hands pick her up and cradle her and rock her back and forth as if she were an infant. And granddaughter felt warmth entering her heart, her belly and her bones. Just as suddenly as her sobbing had begun, it ceased. She felt a lightness in her heart and strength in her limbs. She was standing on her feet now, stroking the cheeks and the forehead of her dear, dead grandmother.

Granddaughter has become a grandmother many times now. She has taken her children and her grandchildren across her own broad lap. She has cradled them with her strong, skillful arms, she has laughed and cried with them, she has sung to them and she has stroked them, whispering, "My little ones, listen well. Grandmother's spirit is all around us. She is in the wind and in the trees. She is in the valleys and the hills. Grandmother's spirit hands play with the fish in the streams and light the fire in the hearth. She is always there when we are with warm friends, when we taste delicious food, and whenever there is carefree laughter or salty tears are shed. No matter where we are, grandmother is never far away. And whenever we need her, we can simply shut our eyes and feel her holding us so very close."

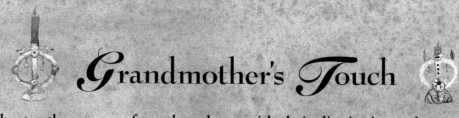

Grandmother's Touch

This story celebrates the power of touch and the continuity of life. When grandmother touches granddaughter she brings to her the love and wisdom of generations. When we touch our children, whether it is with the sound of our voice, our words, a look or in the way we hold and stroke, we imprint both the past and the future. In our touch we carry the way we have been touched. We carry generational messages and values. In turn the cells of our children's bodies carry our messages all through their lives and so as our children grow into adulthood their sense of well-being and self-esteem are formed by the sensory messages we give them, and they in turn pass these messages on to their children.

When grandmother listens she listens beneath the fear into the bones of her grandchild. This is the kind of listening that is needed for children to know they are being received and respected. When children are listened to in this way, they can learn to know what is in their bones. They come to know their ancestral gifts. Then they can learn to listen both to their own needs and to the needs of others. They can ask and give in a respectful way.

When we touch our children with attentiveness and care and we listen to their conscious and subconscious needs and desires we give them a most sacred gift. They learn their place in the universe. In this way, we not only nourish them so they can meet their life with their dignity intact but we nourish the emotional waters of many generations to come. The ripples become waves.

For Mexicans, the spirits of previous generations safeguard and nourish present and future generations in a way that is not just "imagined," but deeply felt and known. Mexicans believe that the spirits of the dead are always near. When a relative or a friend dies, even though the loved ones left behind feel grief and loss, there is a knowledge that their beloved is never far away. A delicate curtain divides the worlds of the living from the dead. Often people can communicate silently and intuitively with their dead relatives and friends. They can sense and sometimes even see and hear the spirits of the dead in their everyday lives. So intimate is their connection with the dead that Mexicans celebrate yearly The Day of the Dead to commemorate both life and death and the eternal life of the soul.

This story honors the Mexican people's deep belief in the soul of the individual surviving death. It also honors the values of indigenous peoples in that grandmother's presence endures after her death not only as an individual spirit, as Mexicans would embrace her, but as an essence of nature.

Barbara Soros